Penguin Post
Debi Gliori

To postpeople
everywhere, but
especially for
Derek and Davey
and everybody at
Haddington
Post Office.
D. G.

Picture Corgi Books

Milo was the youngest in a long line of Penguin Post penguins.

But he wasn't going to be the youngest for long... Mum had laid an Egg, and soon there would be another little penguin in the Post Office.

Milo wasn't sure how he felt about this.

"When will it hatch?" said Milo.

"Any day now," said Milo's mum.

But the Egg still hadn't hatched when Milo's mum had to go on a food-finding expedition.

That meant somebody had to sit on the Egg. And that meant that somebody *else* had to deliver the mail.

"You sit on the Egg,"
said Milo's dad.

"No, I want to deliver the mail," said Milo, tipping over the bag and grabbing a large parcel.

With a sigh, Milo's dad laid the Egg down and stuffed the mail back into the bag. Milo read the address on the parcel:

Ursula Major
11 GlacierGlade
The Pole
BR5 5RR

Milo set off across the ice until he reached the gate of number 11. He watched as Mrs Major opened her parcel. It seemed to be full of snow.

"What are these feathers for?" asked Milo, chasing a handful across the garden.

"I'm going to fill a quilt for Baby Bear with them," explained Mrs Major. "How's the Egg?"

"Not hatched yet," said Milo.

The next parcel was soft and squishy and absolutely enormous. The label read:

Mama Oose
Treetops
Skating Lane
The Pole
SL1 PPY

Slipping and sliding, Milo made his way uphill to "Treetops". Mama Oose was waiting for him.

"At last," she said. "Baby Mooseline will be so pleased. How's the Egg, by the way?"

"It's still an egg," said Milo, hauling the parcel inside.

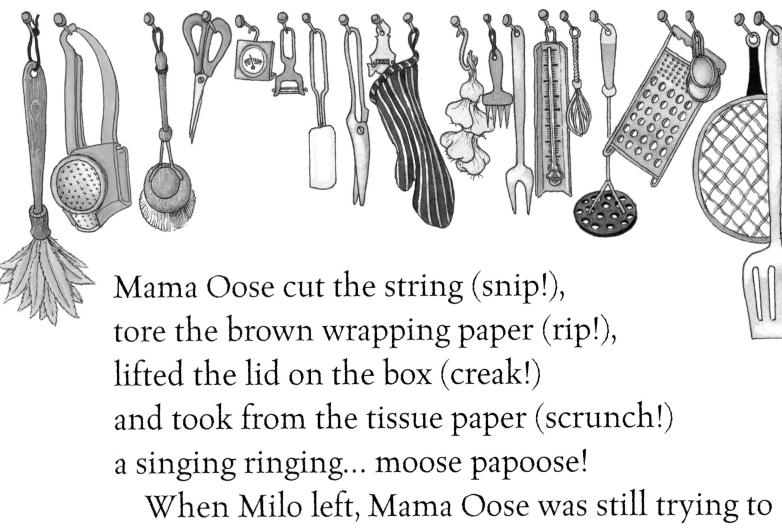

Mama Oose cut the string (snip!),
tore the brown wrapping paper (rip!),
lifted the lid on the box (creak!)
and took from the tissue paper (scrunch!)
a singing ringing... moose papoose!
When Milo left, Mama Oose was still trying to
work out how to put Mooseline into the papoose.

The next package
was quite small

and was addressed to:

BUZZINESS POST

Bee U Tiffle
Vanity Hive
The Buzzwalk
The Pole
BU2 2ZZ

It was quite a long way
to Vanity Hive, so Milo
took the shortcut.

"For me!" squeaked Mrs Tiffle, ripping open the package as soon as Milo handed it to her.
Out fell a tiny...zzzleepsuit.

Mrs Tiffle tutted. "It's the wrong colour. Baby Tiffany would look like a hairy raspberry in this. How's the Egg?"

Milo sighed. "It hasn't hatched yet."

The next parcel was a most peculiar shape. Milo read the label and groaned.

The Cool Cat
Dustbin No. 8
1 Chilled Hill
The Pole
ME1 0OW

Cool Cat wasn't the problem. It was Cool Cat's kittens. They were awful. They scratched and squeaked and miaowed all day long. Milo hoped his Egg wouldn't do that. When he reached No. 8, Milo put the parcel on the dustbin lid and ran. Very fast.

The sky was growing dark and Milo wanted to go home. He peered into his mailbag. Only two more parcels to deliver. He pulled out a small box addressed to:

Stella Polaris
Over The Pole
The Milky Way
The Cosmos
The Universe

Milo sighed. That was a long way away. But the mail had to get through.

So he walked across the ice, through the forest and up the rickety rope-ladder to the lonely place in the sky where Stella Polaris lived.

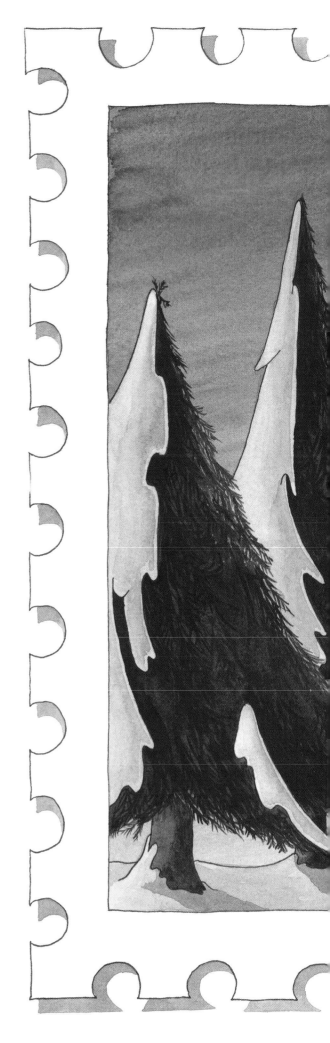

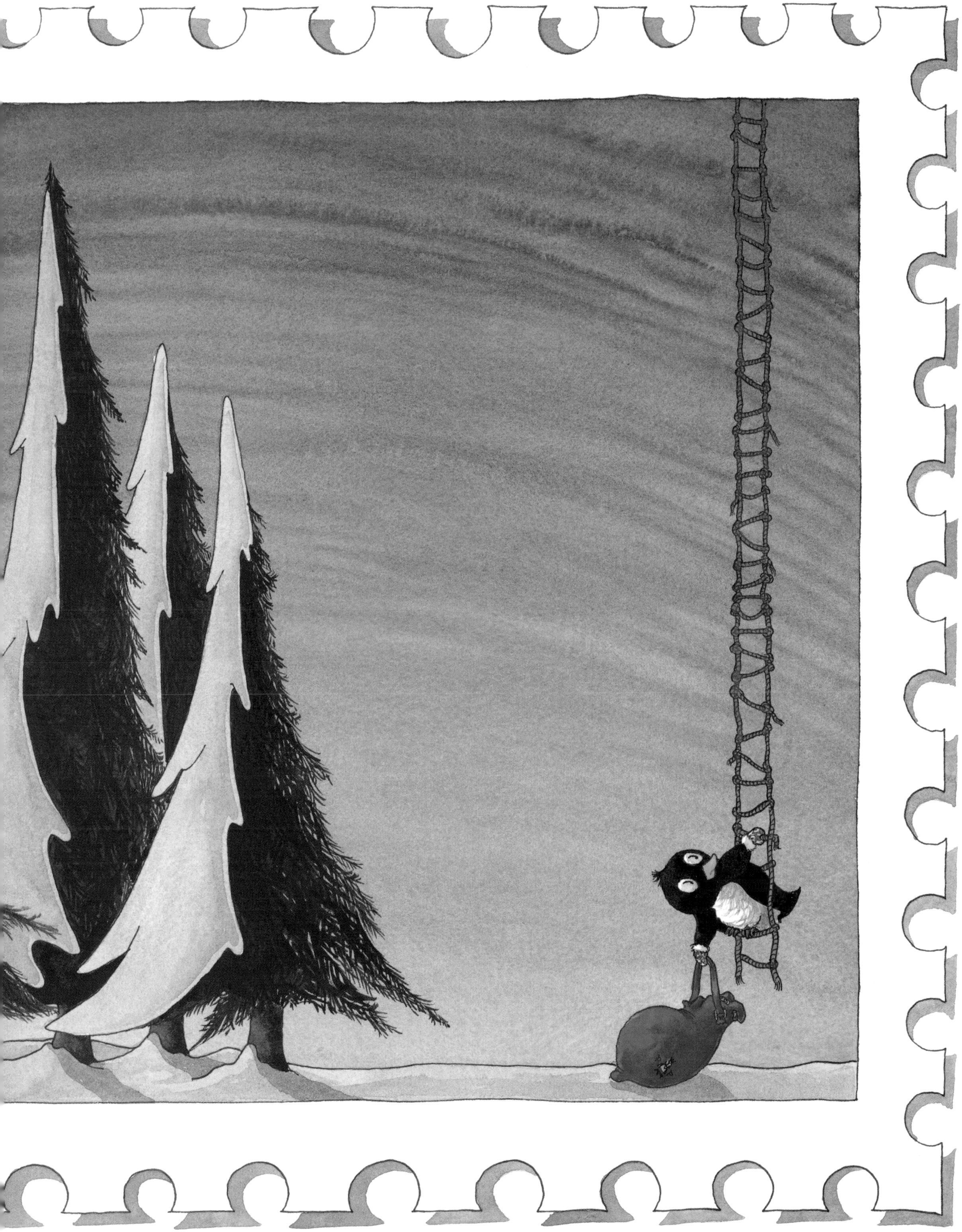

"Miss Polaris!" he called. "I have something for you."
"Thank you, Milo," she said. "I hope this is what I
think it is. I've been waiting such a long time." Stella
Polaris opened the box. Inside was a tiny glass bottle.

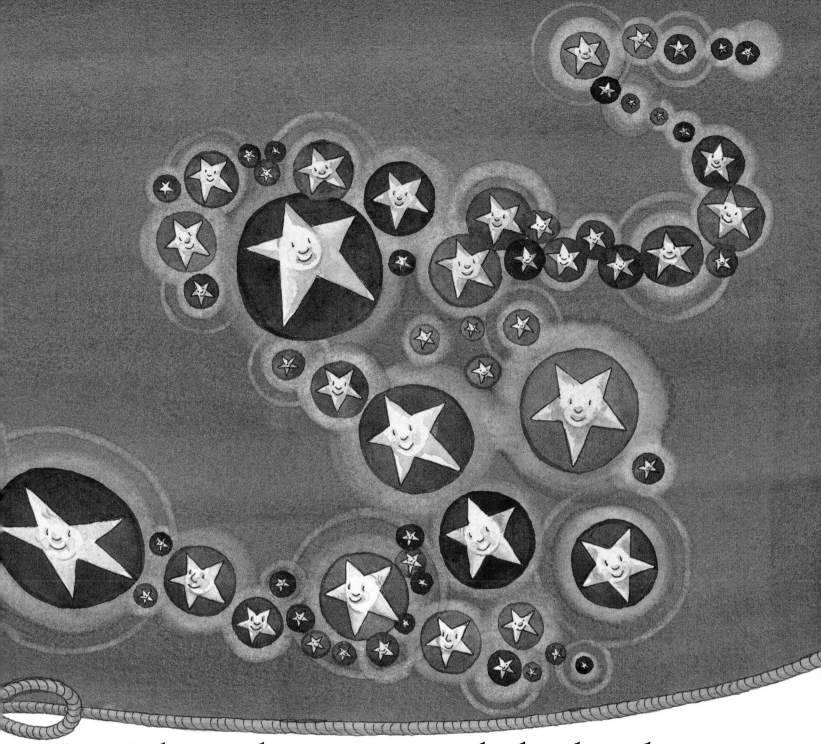

"It is!" she cried, unstoppering the bottle and sprinkling the contents across the sky. Milo rubbed his eyes. In front of him the darkness was peppered with little lights as the sky filled with thousands of baby stars.

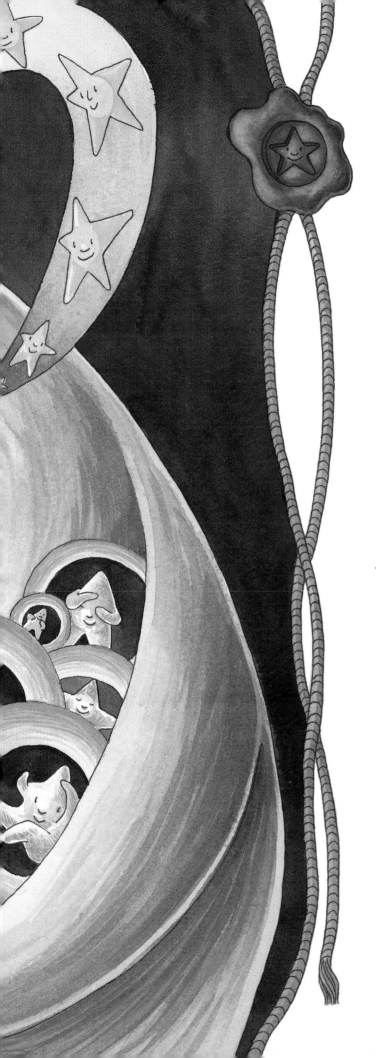

"Thank you so much for delivering my babies, Milo," Stella Polaris said. "What a star you are! Make a wish – any wish – and it will come true."

Milo watched Stella Polaris hug her babies tight, and then something gave a loud

C R A C K !

Milo peeked inside the mailbag. *The Egg!*

Suddenly Milo knew exactly what to wish for — to be back home with his family...

with the Egg held safely in his arms.

"Special Delivery!" he called.

"For us?" said Milo's dad. "I *love* surprises in the post. Let's unwrap it."

"I think it's unwrapping itself," said Milo.

"I'm back!" called Milo's mum, coming over for a hug.

"How's the Egg?"

"It's a *boy!*" said Milo.

"Good heavens!" said Milo's dad, reading the label on the parcel he'd been trying to hatch all day. "For a very special Big Brother. Now who in the world could *that* be...?"

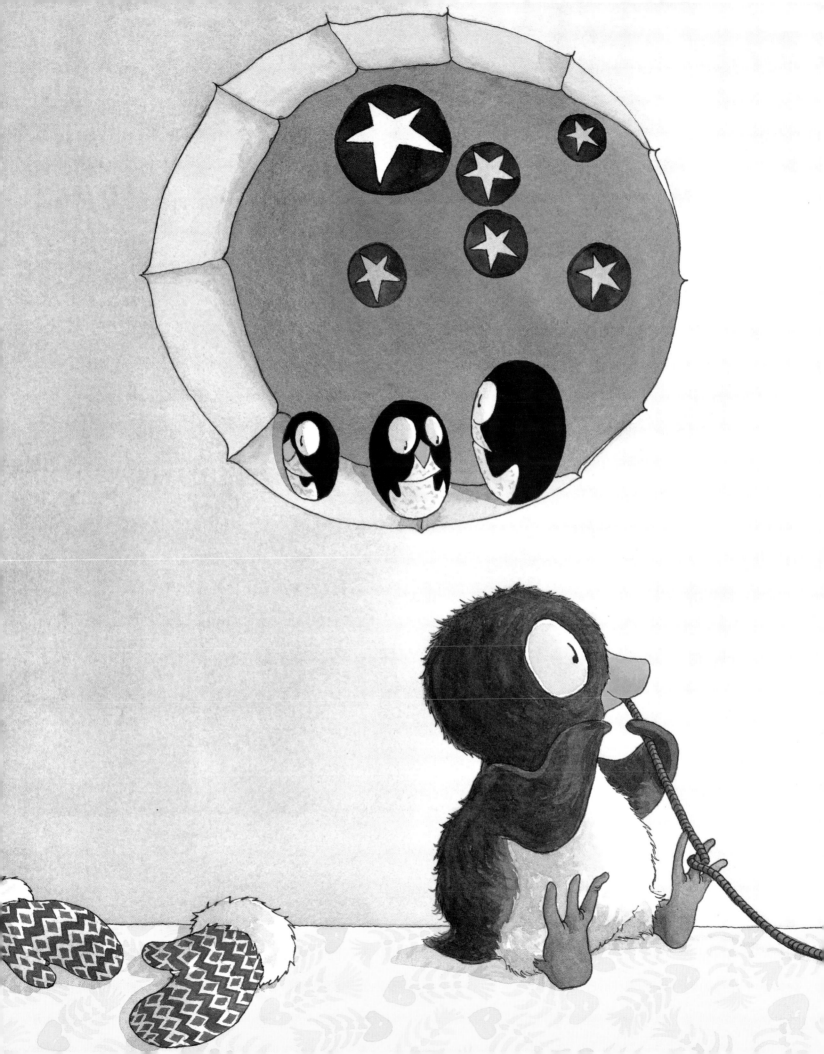

for a very special
Big Brother!
love from Mrs Major,
Mama Oose,
Mrs. Tiffley Cool Cat and
Stella Polaris

PENGUIN POST
A PICTURE CORGI BOOK 0 552 54695 X

First published in Great Britain by Doubleday,
an imprint of Random House Children's Books

Doubleday edition published 2002
Picture Corgi edition published 2003

1 3 5 7 9 10 8 6 4 2

Copyright © Debi Gliori, 2002
Designed by Ian Butterworth

Picture Corgi Books are published by Random House Children's Books,
61–63 Uxbridge Road, London W5 5SA,
a division of The Random House Group Ltd,
in Australia by Random House Australia (Pty) Ltd,
20 Alfred Street, Milsons Point, Sydney, NSW 2061, Australia,
in New Zealand by Random House New Zealand Ltd,
18 Poland Road, Glenfield, Auckland 10, New Zealand,
and in South Africa by Random House (Pty) Ltd,
Endulini, 5A Jubilee Road, Parktown 2193, South Africa

THE RANDOM HOUSE GROUP Limited Reg. No. 954009
www.kidsatrandomhouse.co.uk

A CIP catalogue record for this book is available from the British Library.

Printed in Singapore